MAPPED OUT!

THE SEARCH FOR SNOOKUMS

by Carol Baicker-McKee • Illustrations by Traci O'Very Covey

NOTE TO DETECTIVES

Navigation is concerned with **finding the way**. Your mission, should you choose to accept it, is to navigate:

1) a city (using maps, directories, and examination of your surroundings); and

2) a mystery (using observation, deduction, and inference).

But don't worry if you aren't already a navigational pro; you'll have the best blind guide around—Ms. Bianca Beare! She won't steer you wrong. Good luck!

GIBBS·SMITH
P
PUBLISHER

SALT LAKE CITY

First edition
00 99 98 97 5 4 3 2 1

Text copyright © 1997 by Carol Baicker-McKee
Illustration copyright © 1997 by Traci O'Very Covey

Design by Traci O'Very Covey

Printed and bound in China

Library of Congress Cataloging-in-Publication Data
Baicker-McKee, Carol, 1958-
        Mapped out! : the search for Snookums / Carol
Baicker-McKee
Illustrated by Traci O'Very Covey. --1st ed.
            p.   cm.
        Summary: The reader must use the accompanying
map and follow clues in order to help Bianca Beare, a blind
detective, rescue a rare pet iguana from kidnappers.
        ISBN 0-87905-788-2
        [1. Map reading--Fiction. 2. Mystery and detective
stories.]
I. O'Very Covey, Traci, 1960- ill. II. Title.
PZ7.B1436 Map   1997
[Fic]--dc20   96-27680
                                            CIP
                                            AC

BIANCA BEARE: World-renowned blind detective. She solves most of her cases from the comfort of her specially constructed rocking chair. She loves root beer, chocolate, reptiles, knitting—and you. She hates crime. When she's on the case, criminals beware.

EYEBALLS: That's you, reader. Bright, energetic, attractive—but I hardly need to tell you all of this. You're spending your summer working for the ingenious detective Bianca Beare. She has affectionately nicknamed you "Eyeballs" because you see what her blind eyes cannot. Use those sharp eyeballs on the maps and directories, and you and Ms. B. can solve this case.

LON STORI: The client. Hopscotcher extraordinaire and pet-sitter ordinaire. He was supposed to be caring for his grandmother's menagerie, including a certain rare iguana.

SNOOKUMS: The victim. *Iguana pukapukanesis* or Pukapukan iguana, an endangered species and Lon's grandmother's favorite pet. He looks fierce, but he's really a sweetheart (at least that's what you hope when you have to fetch him).

THE BAD GUYS: Sorry, but I'm certainly not going to tell you about them here! Solve the case and find out about them for yourself.

GRANNY STORI: If you do your job in a timely fashion, you'll never actually meet her. That's probably a good thing, given the mood she's likely to be in once she hears what's happened to Snookums.

THE CASE

TIME: 9:23 A.M., MONDAY, AUGUST 24.
PLACE: PARLOR/OFFICE OF BIANCA BEARE, DETECTIVE.

"What a quiet morning," you think, stifling a yawn. "Too quiet."

You and Ms. Beare are winding yarn. Somehow you'd expected that spending summer vacation working for a famous detective would entail a little more excitement, a little more action. Ms. B. has solved 28 cases this summer—every one without even leaving her specially constructed rocking chair. Your contributions have been, well, nothing to brag about.

"Stop yawning and get the door, Eyeballs, dear. Someone's about to ring the bell," says Ms. Beare. Her hearing is quite good—almost as sharp as her mind.

You open the door. A panting teenager stumbles in, clutching an envelope in one hand and a leash with no pet attached in the other.

"I've got to see Bianca Beare," he gasps. "At once!"

Typical client—upset, in a hurry, and a bit odd. You show him in.

"Ms. Beare," he begs, "you've got to help me find Snookums!"

"I'm sorry," Ms. B. snaps. "This is a detective agency, not a dating service. Try learning to dance. That often helps."

DETECTIVE SUPPLY CHECKLIST

- ☐ Notepad
- ☐ Pencil with eraser
- ☐ Calculator (optional)
- ☐ Brain (not optional)

"No, no, you don't understand," says the guy. "Snookums isn't a girl; he's a lizard. And he's been petnapped!"

Now he's got Ms. B.'s attention. If there is one thing that Ms. B. loves as much as root beer, chocolates, and knitting, it's reptiles.

"I-I-I can pay you," says the young man. "Fifty thousand dollars, if you can get him back by 5:00 tonight."

Now he's really got her attention. Fifty thousand bucks will buy a lot of chocolate.

"Eyeballs," commands Ms. Beare. "Fetch our client a root beer."

"Let me explain," says the guy. "My name is Lon Stori, and my grand—"

"Lon Stori!" Ms. B. interrupts. "Any relation to Scari Stori, the naturalist?"

Lon nods. "She's my grandmother."

"Hey! I know who you are, too!" you say. "Didn't you anchor the Spittsburgh Junior

High hopscotch team last year? The one that won the state title?"

"Yeah," says Lon. "But," he adds morosely, "I may have hopped my last match."

"What!" you exclaim. "Why?"

"My grandmother hired me to pet-sit her rare Pukapukan iguana, Snookums. She's trying to save those lizards from extinction, and she's gone to Pukapuka to find a mate for Snookums. Her last words to me before she left were, 'If anything happens to my Snooks, Lon darling, you'll be a nice picnic for my piranhas.' And now this happens!" Lon moans. "She gets back about 5:00 tonight. I'm fish food for sure!"

"We'll see," says Ms. B. "What happened?"

"I was taking Snookums for his morning walk. As usual, we went to my favorite park," says Lon. "It's got these awesome new hopscotch courts—composite surface, electronic line detectors, glow-in-the-dark paint for night matches—really something.

"Some guy challenged me to a little one-on-one. I said no; I had to take care of Snookums. Then this sweet-looking old lady said, 'Go on, sweetie. I'll watch the little darling.' The court was so tempting, I said sure.

"After a few minutes, I looked over to see how Snookums was doing—and they were gone! Then I noticed his leash on a bench with this taped to it."

Lon hands you an envelope. You read the enclosed letter aloud.

 Remove the letter from the envelope marked "Sucker," and read page 1.

You whistle. "They're serious."

"Yes, they are. And not very polite," says Ms. B. "Where are you going to get this kind of money, young man?"

"Granny left an account with $50,000 for Snookums' expenses while she was gone. So far I've only had to spend about $500, mostly on pistachio ice cream—Snookums' favorite."

"I know what the note says," Ms. Beare says, "but maybe you *should* call the police."

"I can't risk it," wails Lon. "The petnappers say they'll kill him! We're talking about an endangered species! I'll be one if anything happens to Snookums!"

Ms. Beare begins to rock vigorously while humming the theme song from *Gilligan's Island.*

Go to Munny Farm Mall. Further instructions are on the back of this note.

SuckeR

"What's she doing?" asks Lon, confused.

"Shhhhh," you whisper. "Ms. B. is thinking."

Ms. Beare abruptly rocks forward. "Eyeballs," she commands. "Get the map of Spittsburgh from the atlas file. You've got work to do."

Work! You're so excited. And nervous, too. You fetch the map.

Get out the map of Spittsburgh packaged with the book.

"Do you know how to navigate a city with a map, Eyeballs?" Ms. Beare asks.

You shake your head, then realize even Ms. B. can't hear those neurons rattling. "I'm a bit rusty," you admit.

"First, unfold it," says Ms. B.

There. Not too bad. You only mangle it a little.

"Now," says Ms. B. "Get oriented. Find the compass rose. It's a little circle thing with letters N, S, E, and W. On most standard maps, N, which stands for north, is toward the top of the page; S, for south, is toward the bottom; E, for east, is to the right; and W, for west, is to the left."

Lon leans over your shoulder. "Why is the map divided into all these little squares, Ms. B.?"

"Those help you locate specific places on the map when used with the indexes. If my memory serves me correctly, the Spittsburgh map has the indexes on the flip side."

You turn the map over. Yes, there are the "Street Index" and the "Index to Places of Interest."

"Eyeballs," says Ms. B., "I'll tell you how to use these features while you figure out

how to get to Munny Farm Mall. You're going to pick up the ransom."

Yes! The ransom!

"First, look at the 'Index to Places of Interest.' It's arranged by categories. Find the category labeled something like 'Shopping' or 'Retail Areas.'"

Aha! "Shopping" it is.

"Now, find the listing for Munny Farm Mall. Do you see it?"

"Yes," you say. "And I see a letter followed by a number—H-5."

"Excellent," says Ms. B. "Turn to the map side again. Find the square that falls in the column marked 'H' and in the row marked '5.' Then look for the Munny Farm Mall."

You do it! You are going to be a great detective. You . . .

"Now, dearie," says Ms. B, "can you figure out how to get there from my place?"

Sheepishly, you admit that you can't. "Your address is 622 Teddy Lane," you say. "But I don't know how to get to the mall from here. Someone always drives me there."

"Okay, Eyeballs. What you need to do now is use the Street Index to find my place. The index is arranged in alphabetical order. Find Teddy Lane and then see what the grid coordinates are."

You find it: E-5, almost due west from the mall.

"Now, figure out the best route," says Ms. B. "The ransom note says to go to the South Entrance. Remember to pay attention to one-way streets, because you'll need to ride your bike. You can tell one-way streets on the map because they have little arrows."

"Well," you say. "I have several choices."

Try to plan a route yourself. Then read on, using the map to follow the directions given. How did you do? (There are several workable routes.)

"I think I'll turn right out of your drive, and take an immediate left onto Michael. I'll stay on that until it ends at Fies Boulevard, where I'll turn right. At Ninth Avenue, I'll go right again. After crossing Speed Way, I can turn left into the parking lot by the south end of the mall. That's a pretty direct route. It also avoids golf-cart traffic, going the wrong way on Eighth Avenue or having to travel on Speed Way, which is kind of dangerous on a bike."

"Brilliant brainwork!" Ms. B. beams. "You knew that to avoid getting your rights and lefts confused, you'd have to picture yourself facing the direction you'd be traveling on each street."

She has Lon write you a check to get the ransom money. You tuck the check, the map, and some helpful tips from Ms. B. in one pocket and the ransom note in another. You're off!

Now you know how to do this! Look up the mall on the map again. You will note a page number, printed in a blue circle. Turn now to that page—22. You don't read the pages of this book in the usual order!

You will follow this procedure for other steps in solving the mystery. Correctly following the directions on the map will lead you to a landmark with a page number on it. If you turn to that page and the text doesn't make sense, you will know that you made a mistake. Go back and try again or turn to the end of the book for more help in using the maps and directories.

RETURN SNOOKUMS

"Snookums! Boy, it's great to see you!" You hug him. "What's that you're eating, boy?" You fish a piece of an envelope out of his mouth.

"Yuck! Don't eat paper!" you say as you look around for some place to toss it. No trash cans, so you stick it in your pocket.

"What time is it, Snooks?" you ask. "Yikes! 4:12. We'd better get moving."

You exit the ballpark via the pedestrian walkway.

"Okay, Snooks, I'll just whip out the Spittsburgh map, and—oops! Hey, do you know where you live? I have no idea."

You dash to a pay phone at the market on Atlas Blvd. and call Ms. B. The line is busy; too bad you haven't been able to talk her into getting call-waiting. You check for a phone book. None there. You call the operator and ask for listings for Scari Stori or Lon Stori. No luck.

You are hopping up and down in a total panic when you suddenly spot one of Ms. B.'s kindly neighbors walking nearby.

"Mr. Hoojy!" you call. "By any chance, do you know Scari Stori, the naturalist?"

Mr. Hoojy stops and greets you. "Scari Stori?" he says. "Why, yes, I do. Not well, but I went to her place a couple of years ago

for a house tour. It was a benefit for the Friends of Fauna. Interesting place; different reptile theme for each room. I was particularly intrigued by the Snapping Turtle Room."

"I need to get to her house pronto," you say. "Do you recall her address?"

"Hmmmm," says Mr. Hoojy. "Can't say that I remember the name of the street, but I think I can direct you from here.

"Let's see. This is Atlas Blvd. You want to walk along here toward Pointless Park until you get to Park Drive. Atlas kind of runs right into it. Keep going in the same direction along Park for a ways. When you get to the main entrance to the park, you'll take a right on that street there. Now, which one is it? One of the numbered ones, I know. Eighth? Ninth?"

"I'm pretty sure that's Ninth," you say, trying to hurry him along.

"Ninth? Okay. Well, anyway, you'll know it because it's right at the park. Then you'll take your second right. Should be a school right about there. Walk along that block until the street ends. Take a left, and walk along that street until it ends. Turn again, heading *away* from downtown.

"In just a short way, there will be a

street heading off to the right. That's Ms. Stori's street. Wish I could remember the name of it. Anyway, her house is in the middle of the block. On the left side, I think. She's got a lizard-shaped door knocker, so you should be able to find it even without the house number. Quite a woman, that Ms. Stori. Bet she'd like your little friend here."

While he tickles Snookums under the chin, you thank him and scribble down his directions. You hurry along, stopping to retrieve your bike at the park. Fortunately, Snookums likes riding in the basket.

Get out the Spittsburgh map. Find the market on Atlas Blvd. and follow Mr. Hoojy's directions. Where do you end up?

Can this be right? There are *no* houses on the left side of the street, and you don't see any lizard knockers anywhere. You run to a nearby pay phone and dial Ms. B.'s number. Oh, good! This time it's ringing.

Turn now to the page number on the spot you've reached on the Spittsburgh map.

6

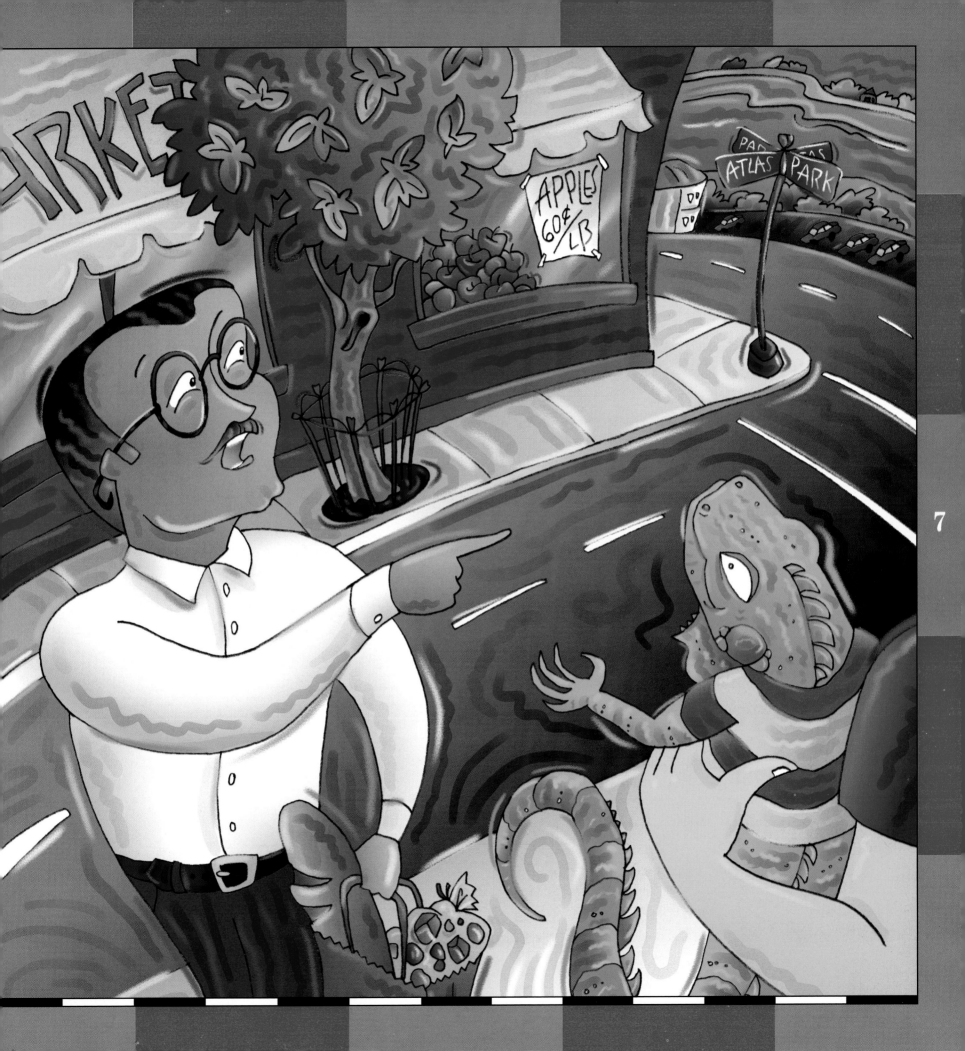

Now what? You open the last note at the park and read:

Okay, okay, we're satisfied that you haven't gone to the police. If an officer had seen you "performing" in the park, they'd have had to take you into protective custody. By the way, you need to work on your crab-walk. Now we're going to send you to the place where we want you to drop the ransom.

Cross the street. Go down into the SPIT station. Here's what you do:

1. Take the Circle Line eastbound for 2 stops.

2. Transfer to the other line you can board at the station you've reached. Head away from Overburb.

3. At the third stop, transfer to the line that has a stop for Columbo Park. Get off at the 2nd stop past Columbo Park.

4. Transfer to the line that has a stop for 4th Avenue, but head toward Everland.

5. Go one stop, and exit to the building, not the street. Go to the Information Desk. Ask for a message for "Smartypants."

A trip by SPIT! You've never taken the Spittsburgh subway (or SPIT, as it is more commonly known) by yourself. You leave your bike locked at the park, dash down the steps into the station—and feel bewildered. This does seem to be the Circle Line,

**BIANCA BEARE
DETECTIVE AGENCY**
622 TEDDY LANE
SPITTSBURGH NP 00146

Eyeballs Dearie,

You may have to ride SPIT at some point. Don't be surprised if you find the system confusing. SPIT can make even seasoned detectives feel wet behind the ears. But with these notes and a copy of the subway map, I know your first-rate mind will figure out SPIT.

First, you need to know about **lines.** A subway line is nothing but a group of stops that the same train will go to. (On a map, different lines are usually shown by different colors or different symbols. This SPIT guide uses both.) You can't go from a stop on one line to a stop on a different line without finding a station where you can **transfer**, or change from one line to the other. Stops where you can transfer are called **interchanges**. So, on SPIT, you can go from Desmond to Pain Gym on the Heart Line, but to go from Desmond to Durrell Zoo, you'd have to take the Heart Line to Botanical Gardens, then transfer to the Circle Line.

Now, another tricky thing about subway maps is trying to figure out how the subway map compares to the street map. SPIT stops are marked on the Spittsburgh street map with the symbol: 🌢. Stops or stations are usually named for streets or landmarks near them. This information is important, because subway maps aren't to scale, and they tend to show stops laid out in straighter lines than they actually are. For example, if you drew lines on the Spittsburgh street map between the three stops Columbo Park, 8th Ave., and Francis Blvd., you would draw an upside-down V. The SPIT map, though, shows a straight line connecting these stops on the Triangle Line.

The last problem is figuring out where to go in the station. Say you managed to figure out that you need the Square Line to go from the Shopping District to Nottingham. Then, you even got the machine to cough up your token, and you got through the turnstile without getting stuck! You'd still need to know one more thing: which platform do you want? What's a platform anyway? Well, the platform is where you wait for the train. You have to use the map and your brain to figure out which platform to use. In this example, you'd want the platform that says "To Beverly Mounds," even though you aren't going there. That's because Nottingham is between Shopping District and the last stop, Beverly Mounds. You do not want the platform that says "Art Museum;" that's the last stop in the *other* direction. (On some systems, the platforms show directions differently, like "Southbound" or "Uptown.") Good luck, Eyeballs!

Yours,

Ms. B.

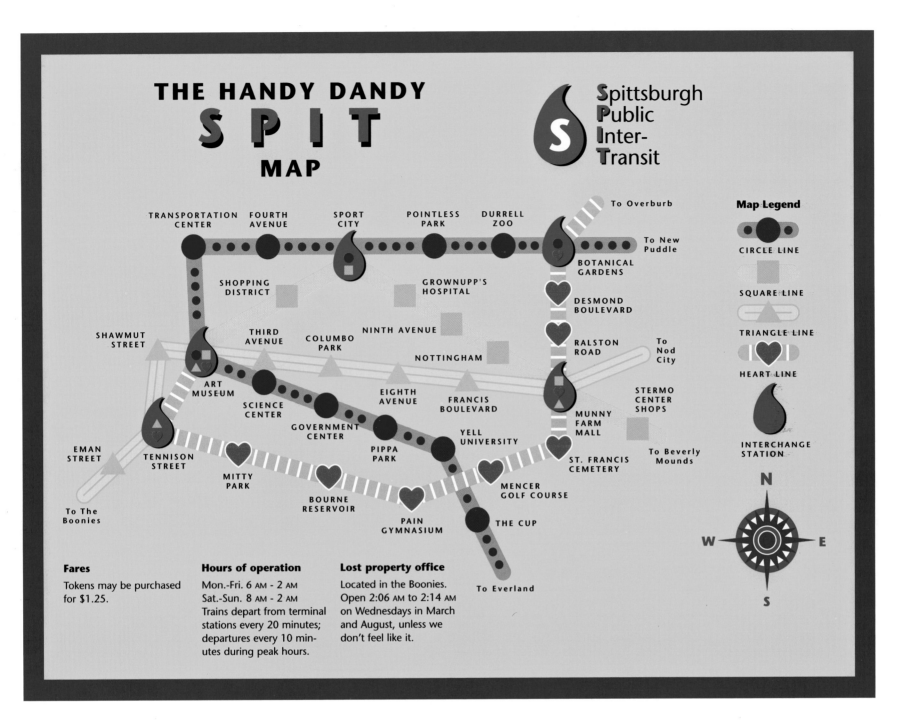

THE HANDY DANDY SPIT MAP

Spittsburgh Public Inter-Transit

Map Legend

CIRCLE LINE

SQUARE LINE

TRIANGLE LINE

HEART LINE

INTERCHANGE STATION

To Overburb

To New Puddle

TRANSPORTATION CENTER

FOURTH AVENUE

SPORT CITY

POINTLESS PARK

DURRELL ZOO

BOTANICAL GARDENS

SHOPPING DISTRICT

GROWNUPP'S HOSPITAL

DESMOND BOULEVARD

SHAWMUT STREET

THIRD AVENUE

COLUMBO PARK

NINTH AVENUE

RALSTON ROAD

To Nod City

NOTTINGHAM

STERMO CENTER SHOPS

ART MUSEUM

SCIENCE CENTER

EIGHTH AVENUE

FRANCIS BOULEVARD

MUNNY FARM MALL

EMAN STREET

TENNISON STREET

GOVERNMENT CENTER

YELL UNIVERSITY

ST. FRANCIS CEMETERY

To Beverly Mounds

MITTY PARK

PIPPA PARK

To The Boonies

BOURNE RESERVOIR

PAIN GYMNASIUM

MENCER GOLF COURSE

THE CUP

To Everland

N S E W

Fares

Tokens may be purchased for $1.25.

Hours of operation

Mon.-Fri. 6 AM - 2 AM
Sat.-Sun. 8 AM - 2 AM
Trains depart from terminal stations every 20 minutes; departures every 10 minutes during peak hours.

Lost property office

Located in the Boonies. Open 2:06 AM to 2:14 AM on Wednesdays in March and August, unless we don't feel like it.

---

but there is no sign for eastbound trains. One says "To Art Museum" and the other says "To New Puddle."

You take a couple of deep breaths. Ms. B. says that's the best thing to do when you're confused. Suddenly, you remember that before you set off, Ms. B. gave you a copy of the "Handy Dandy SPIT Map" and some

notes on how to use the system. You sit down on a bench to read her notes and study the subway map.

After reading Ms. B.'s notes, you find that you're feeling much better; you have even figured out which platform to use. You study the SPIT guide, plan your journey, and head off to drop the ransom.

Find the SPIT stop that is across the street from the park where you are now. Then use the subway map on this page to figure out the next destination in the bad guys' note. When you know what it is, find it on the Spittsburgh street map. (Using the street map indexes may save you time and effort.) The page number printed at that location will direct you to the next page in the book.

AT POINTLESS PARK

You find a note for "Birdbrain" taped to the main entrance gate. You grab it and read:

You'd better not have gone to the police. We're watching you to see if you're being straight with us. If you follow our instructions exactly, we'll tell you where to leave the ransom:

1. Bunny hop (yes, we mean it) along the path leading from the main entrance toward the badminton courts.

2. When the path ends, gallop westward to an equipment shed with 3 trash cans.

3. Skip to the back of the shed. Across the path from there, you'll see a sign.

4. Look for the attraction that is about halfway between the sign and the carousel. Duck-walk over. Your next instructions will be tacked to this site.

You lock your bike in the rack and start bunny hopping down the path. People are looking at you, but you don't care. After all, you are a trained professional.

 Follow the petnappers' directions using the picture map of the park. Lift the flap showing the site you reach. (If you don't see your destination, you'll know you made a mistake. Try again!) Follow the instructions under the flap. You'll lift the flaps for three steps at the park. But watch out! Some of the flaps are red herrings—tricks that will send you the wrong way!

At the last destination you reach, there should be a sign with numbers on it. Find the *last* digit on the sign. That is the page number you should turn to next.

HANDY TIP:
Remember to *reverse* right and left when moving from the *top* of the map toward the *bottom*.

? * Need help following this instruction?
Remember, you can turn to the back of the book any time you need assistance reading the maps and directories or following directions.

HOPSCOTCH COURTS

PICNIC TABLE

EQUIPMENT SHED #1

THE TREE HOUSE

KICKBALL FIELD A

THE SAND PIT

AGAIN

"Beare Detective Agency, Bianca Beare speaking."

"Ms. B.! It's me!" you say, shifting Snookums, who is eating the phone cord. "I've got Snookums, but I'm lost! I don't know how to get him home!"

"Slow down, dear," says Ms. B. soothingly. "It will work out. You say you've got Snookums? Then you've done splendidly! Plenty of time left. Now, where are you?"

"Uh, some park," you say. "There's a sign: Schmitz Park. I got directions at the market on Atlas from your neighbor, Mr. Hoojy. They seemed right—I saw all the landmarks he mentioned—until I ended up here! This is obviously not right."

"Tell me the directions he gave you, dear," says Ms. B.

Quickly, you read back your notes.

Ms. B. says, "Well, Mr. Hoojy was quite close, but you wanted your second *left* off Ninth, not the second right. Just retrace your steps to that point, and then follow his directions and you'll be fine. Remember, reversing directions is tricky—you have to do each step the opposite. For example, since you turned right onto Schmitz Circle, now you'll turn left off of it." Ms. B. tells you the correct address, which you scribble on a piece of paper in your notebook.

"Come on, Snooks," you say, hanging up. "I hope you're a speed demon." Snookums leans over and eats the page from your notebook with Ms. Stori's address.

"Hey! Spit that out! I didn't memorize the address!"

Snookums burps. You try to call Ms. B. back, but the line is busy again!

"Rats! What was the street name? Something like Cow or Call."

You check the street index, but no luck.

"Never mind," you sigh. "I think I have enough information to find your home now."

You climb on your bike and begin pedaling back to where you turned off Ninth.

 On the Spittsburgh map, try to follow the directions in reverse, using your "notes." It's harder than you might think. Turn to the notes at the end of the book if you have trouble. Which step might be especially difficult to reverse in real life? (There is a shorter route you could have taken, too. Can you spot it?)

On Ninth, you quickly locate the second *left* off Ninth that you should have taken. From there, you follow the rest of Mr. Hoojy's directions.

Now you should be able to locate Ms. Stori's house. It *is* on the left side of the street. To figure out the number of the next page in the book, look for the number printed on Ms. Stori's house on the map.

WARNING: Remember that right and left can be tricky! Think about which way you are heading on Ms. Stori's street.

THE CHASE IS ON!

13

You dash back upstairs and find Officers Dimble and Laggin trying to decide what to do with the carton of melting pistachio ice cream.

"We can't throw it away because we need the carton. And we can't put it down the garbage disposal," explains Officer Laggin, "because we know it's bad to dispose of evidence."

"I'll take care of it," you say, glad that you always carry a spoon in your back pocket. "But right now we need to get going. I've figured out where the petnappers should be. If we hurry, we'll be in time to capture those vermin!"

While Officer Dimble drives and Officer Laggin navigates, you concentrate on eating. Man, all that detecting sure can work up an appetite. Even for pistachio ice cream. Why couldn't Snookums have liked triple chocolate fudge chunk?

"Um, Eyeballs?" says Officer Laggin after several minutes.

"Are we there already?" you ask.

"Well, not exactly. Actually, we're lost," she admits.

"Hopelessly lost," says Dimble.

"Not hopelessly," you say, getting out your map. "Navigating's definitely something I can do. What street are we on?"

"I'm not quite sure," says Laggin. "The sign seems to be missing. Can you still figure out where we are?"

"Probably not," says Dimble. "Might as well head back to the police station."

 1. Study the illustration of your current location. Several landmarks are visible. 2. Use the indexes to look up the landmarks. Pinpoint your probable location on the street map. 3. Plan the *shortest* route to your destination. (You'll want to pull in the *drop-off drive* in front, not into the garage.) 4. Count the number of streets you must travel on to get there (counting the one you are on, but *not* counting the driveway as a street).*
5. Add that total to the number on your *current* location to find the next page in the book.

*There is more than one possible route.

THE SEARCH FOR
EVIDENCE

You arrive at the petnappers' place, which turns out to be an apartment building. A police car is already parked out front. You ring the bell by "Roach, R., and Less-Roach, R.," and an officer buzzes you in.

"Did you arrest them yet?" you ask.

"No," says Officer Laggin. "No one's home. What's worse, we think they're planning to be gone a long time. There were notes by the front door telling the milkman and paper carrier to halt deliveries 'until further notice.' Also, the phone is disconnected."

Officer Dimble shows you the notes and says, "Guess we won't get them this time. Might as well head back to the station."

You scan the apartment, trying to think logically like Ms. B. would.

"Just a minute," you say. "We shouldn't leave yet. I think I see some clues."

With your encouragement, the police officers decide to conduct a thorough search. They ask you to assist them.

SEARCH THE APARTMENT SCENE

There are at least

a. 4 clues that Snookums may have been in the apartment;

b. 4 clues that the suspects obtained the ransom items (the green jelly beans, the sunglasses, the dictionary, and the check);

c. 3 clues that the suspects could have been involved in picking up the ransom and returning Snookums;

d. 3 clues about a trip the suspects have been planning; and

e. 5 clues about what the suspects look like (to help identify them later).

Some of the clues are readily visible. Search carefully and use your head. (You may also notice some evidence that Snookums is not the first pet these guys have napped.)

When you have completed your hunt for clues, turn to the next spread. You can discover the correct page number by:

1. looking for numbers in the following places:
   a. above the tub and next to the sink
   b. on the *2nd* shelf in the cabinet over the sink and near the fridge
   c. just above the bookcase and below a picture of an animal; then

2. adding each *digit* together.

?

Need help figuring out what you're looking for?

Just check your notebook to "refresh" your memory.

You pull up in front of the train station at 7:12. Getting there was no problem once you took over the navigating.

"I still can't figure out how you managed to end up on Carnon," you say to Laggin. "That was totally the wrong direction."

"Well, it was complicated," she says. "There were so many one-way streets. Besides, Dimble turned south when I told him to turn north."

"Did not," says Dimble.

"Did so," says Laggin.

"Guys, guys," you say. "Cut the arguing. I'll teach you both how to navigate when this is over, but right now we need to find those crooks. Let's see, which platform do we want?"

"Holy Train Tracks!" says Dimble. "This looks totally confusing. We'll never figure out where to go in here. We might as well give up. Can you get us back to the police station?"

"Hang on," you say. "It does look complicated, but we'll manage."

The line at the information desk is about a mile long, and the gentleman behind the desk won't let you cut in, not even for police business. So you grab a train timetable and solve the puzzle yourself.

"We know the important facts: they depart Spittsburgh at 7:38 P.M. and arrive in New York at 10:19 A.M.," you say. "So we should be able to figure out which train they are taking. Then we can use the board to find the right track."

GoRail Train Timetable

And leave the chugging to us...

EASTBOUND TRAINS — Read Down | WESTBOUND TRAINS — Read Up

Train Number	1057	8902	2461	1193	1563	0002
Train Name	The Buzzard	The Blue Moon	The Slug	The Racing Rat	The Scooter	The Buzzard
Frequency of Operation	M-W-F	November Only	Tu-Th	Weekdays	Daily	Mon
Cleveland OH	4:02 am	9:07 am	4:37 pm	1:19 am	11:26 pm	Dep 8:07 pm / Ar 7:38 pm
Spittsburgh NP (Ar / Dep)	5:23 am / 7:38 am	6:44 pm / 7:38 pm	5:15 pm / 9:22 pm	7:03 pm / 7:38 pm	3:26 am / 3:27 am	Dep 5:52 pm / Ar 5:51 pm
Bilkes-Warre NP	10:59 pm / 8:52 pm			1:15 am / 3:26 am	5:39 am / 10:19 am	
Pittsburgh PA (Ar / Dep)	9:16 am / 11:09 am			11:30 am / 1:39 pm	5:49 am / 9:02 am	11:41 am
Philadelphia PA (Ar / Dep)		12:03 am / 9:43 am		4:51 pm	10:19 am	Dep 10:19 ar / Ar 9:26 am
Princeton NJ	5:56 pm			10:19 am / 11:43 am	2:57 am	
New York NY (Ar / Dep)	10:19 pm / 10:48 pm	10:19 am / 10:27 am		11:38 pm		6:14 a
Boston MA	1:42 am	1:37 pm				

Use the train schedule to find the name of the train Rancid and Ruth will be taking. (Remember, this is a Monday in August.) Then look at the board to figure out from which track it leaves. When you know the right one, lift the flap by the correct listing to learn the next page number you need. Hurry, the train is already boarding.

SNOOKUMS?

You arrive breathless at Strawberry Field, home of the Spittsburgh Mules kickball team! You hurry to the Will Call window at Gate A and ask for the ticket being held for "Twinkletoes." Paperclipped to the ticket is a note that says:

> The reptile's all yours, Twinkletoes. You'll find him in a seat in the following location:
>
> Level: One alphabet letter past yours.
>
> Section: Yours + 3
>
> Row: 3 less than yours
>
> Seat Number: Yours times 2
>
> Be careful. You wouldn't want to deliver the wrong critter to Ms. Stori.

Wrong critter? Then you look up and see a banner proclaiming:

Lizard Day! First 200 guests accompanied by Scaly 4-Legged Friends will receive a FREE Spittsburgh Mules Kickball Cap autographed by first baseman Komodo "The Dragon" Karate

You *will* have to be extra careful. Rather than waste time finding your seat, you ask for a stadium seating chart. Too bad you can't stay to watch the game. The Mules' ace roller, Rollie Toes, is pitching against the Thumpers' best pitcher, Bob Bowler.

You start to walk in, but the Will Call guy stops you, saying, "Hey, that ticket isn't paid for yet! That'll be $7.50, please."

Sheesh! These petnappers aren't only nasty, they're cheapskates.

18

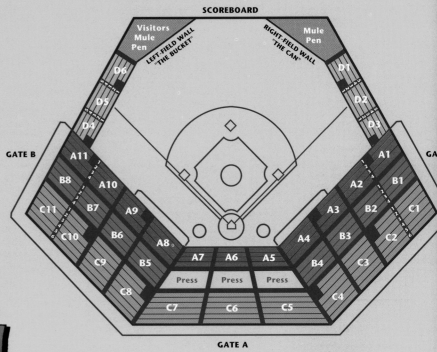

SEATING CHART FOR
STRAWBERRY FIELD
HOME OF THE
SPITTSBURGH MULES

A - Field Boxes

B - Loge Boxes

C - Grandstand

D - Bleachers

"We Kick Back"

IN EACH ROW, SEATS ARE NUMBERED 1–10
MOVING CLOCKWISE

CALL 555-MULE FOR TICKET INFORMATION AND RESERVATIONS

Use the seating chart to locate your seat. Then follow the petnappers' instructions to pinpoint Snookums' seat. Locate the corresponding seat on the facing illustration. It's tricky: the illustration shows only a portion of the stadium. You will have to pay attention to stadium landmarks (e.g., the position of the foul line) to figure out the portion shown. When you find Snookums, turn to the page numbered on his cap.

This is clearly the right place.

Lon throws the door open before you even get to use the lizard knocker. Rats. Snookums leaps into his arms, obviously happy to see a familiar face. He covers Lon with lizard licks.

"Oh, Snookums!" says Lon. "I never thought I'd be so glad to smell your stinky lizard breath.

"Thank you, Eyeballs!" says Lon, turning to you. "I'd be on my way to the fish-food factory shortly if it weren't for you. You were brilliant! Amazing! Stupendous!"

True, true, but what else would anyone expect? "All in a day's work," you reply. "May I use the phone?"

Lon hands you the Gila monster phone.

"Hello, Ms. B.? Eyeballs here. Mission accomplished: Snookums is safely back home," you say. "Should I stay until Ms. Stori returns?"

"Good heavens, no!" says Ms. Beare. "Believe me, you'll want to be well clear by the time that woman finds out what happened. But I don't want you back here, either. The case isn't finished."

You look around: Lon, Snookums, Ms. Stori's house—what's missing?

"My dear Eyeballs," says Ms. Beare, "we haven't nabbed the nappers! We cannot let the kidnapping of an innocent reptile go unavenged, can we?"

Reluctantly you agree. A cold root beer and a few chocolates sure would taste good about now. Even a little yarn-winding sounds tempting; your tootsies are tired.

"One small problem, Ms. B.," you say. "We haven't a clue who did this. I can't exactly run around town stopping strangers and asking, 'Excuse me, but have you kidnapped any reptiles lately?' People might get a bit testy."

"You're right," agrees Ms. B. "Besides, great detectives do not rely on trial and error. We use our keen senses and our trained investigative minds. We must search for clues. Get out your notebook and we'll review everything. You may have overlooked some detail that would give us a clue to the identities of the lizard-nappers."

As you reach into your pocket to pull out your notes, a piece of paper flutters to the ground. You reach over and pick it up. It's the paper—or rather, envelope—that Snookums was chewing at the ballpark. You turn it over, examining it carefully.

"Ms. B.!" you say. "I think I've found an important clue! It's part of an envelope I fished out of Snookums' mouth. On one side, there is a list of the ransom items with a check mark by each one. On the other side, there are names and an address."

"Excellent!" says Ms. B. "Tell me the names and address and I'll send the police right over."

"Uh, one small problem," you say. "Snookums ate a lot of the envelope, and

parts of the names and address are missing. I guess this clue wasn't helpful after all."

"Now, don't give up too soon," says Ms. B. "Use that cunning cranium of yours, Eyeballs. Maybe you can make something of the information you've got."

You think quickly yet deeply. Aha!

"Lon! Fetch me the Spittsburgh white pages."

While Lon tracks down the phone book, you outline your strategy to Ms. B. "I'm going to check the phone book for names beginning with the letters on the envelope. Then I'll see if any of the possibilities has an address that fits with the part that's readable on the envelope."

Use the phone book pages—and logic—to figure out the names and address of the petnappers. Watch out! There are several possibilities, but only one will really fit.

"I've got it!" you shout. You report the names and address.

"Premium detective work, Eyeballs!"

says Ms. B. "It's not conclusive evidence, of course, but I'll send the police right over with a search warrant. You meet them there. Leave your bike with Lon for now, and take the subway. It will be much faster."

You ask Lon for the location of the nearest SPIT stop. He tells you that Granny Stori's neighbors allow them to cut through their backyard to the stop; the nearest station would be much farther if you had to stick to the streets. You head out the back door, studying the SPIT map as you go.

1. Use the Spittsburgh map to find the nearby SPIT station. 2. Then find the petnappers' street on the map. There is a SPIT stop one block southwest of their place. 3. Use the subway map to figure out the route to that stop that involves the *fewest transfers*. 4. Count the number of *stops* and *add* that to the number printed on the petnappers' location. 5. Turn to the page number that equals that *total*.

GETTING THE RANSOM

At the mall, you get right to work following the instructions on the back of the ransom note.

Use the directory on this page to find the first three digits of each number. Then search the illustrations on p. 23 to find the final four digits. Remember, you are viewing the mall from the directory at the south end of the mall.

When you have everything, you quickly add the four numbers. Fortunately, your brain is hitting on all cylinders, and the arithmetic is no problem. (You even remember to check your answer—wouldn't your teacher be proud?!)

Aha! You've got the number. You rush to one of the pay phones (which floor were they on?) to call the petnappers. Your heart is pounding.

Call the petnappers by lifting the pay-phone flap showing the correct number. Be careful—the other phones will send you to the wrong places. When you know your next destination, find it on the map of Spittsburgh, using the Index to Places of Interest. Plan your route as before. When you find the landmark, look for the page number printed on it.

If you do not see the phone number you got, check your addition and/or your searching.

Finally, you call Ms. B. to report in.

"Excellent work, Eyeballs," she says. "Hop on your bike and get moving. But while you're riding, let the back of your mind start working on the clues you have so far. Like, what kind of people would be into green jelly beans, anyway?"

Now turn to the page on the landmark. (Don't forget to return the ransom note to the envelope on page 4.)

THE MUNNY FARM MALL

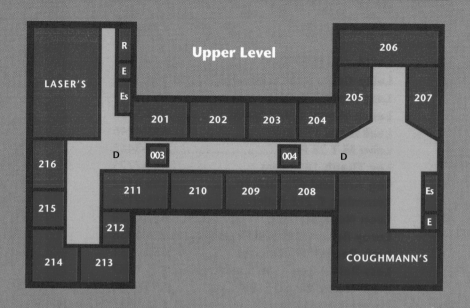

Upper Level

LASER'S

R
E
Es

206
205 207
201 202 203 204
D 003 004 D
216
211 210 209 208
215
212
Es
E
214 213

COUGHMANN'S

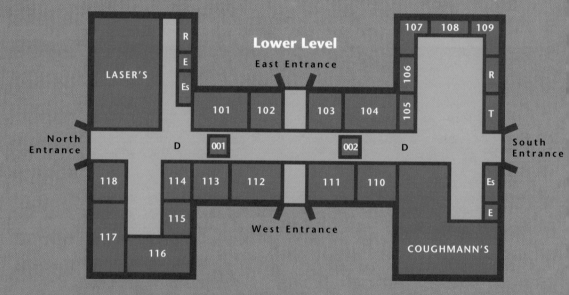

Lower Level

LASER'S

R
E
Es

East Entrance

107 108 109
106
105
R
T
101 102 103 104

North Entrance

D 001 002 D

South Entrance

118 114 113 112 111 110
115
117
Es
E
116

West Entrance

COUGHMANN'S

Map Legend

R = Restrooms
T = Telephones
E = Elevator
Es = Escalator
D = Directory

N E S W

BANKS

216 Checks R Us
112 Second National Bank of Cash
003 Sharky's Savings & Loan
118 The Diss Credit Union

BOOKSTORES

102 The Closed Book: Coffee-table Classics
207 Get A Clue! Mystery Books
204 Mapped Out!: Atlases for Every Occasion
209 The Tongue Shop: Foreign Language Books

CLOTHING

OVERWEAR

203 Heads or Tails: Toilets and Tuxedos
104 Marco's Polos
210 Mutant Jeans
213 No Sweat: Clothes for Couch Potatoes

UNDERWEAR

215 Bloomers for Boomers
002 Down Under Down Undies
211 Knancy's Knickers

DEPARTMENT STORES

Coughmann's
Laser's

EYEWEAR

111 The Red Eye: Crazy-Colored Contacts
004 Make A Spectacle: Do-It-Yourself Bifocals
115 Ruby's Rose-Colored Glasses
001 Shades in All Shades

FOOD COURT

106 Escar-To-Go
109 The Gas Grill: Fried Cabbages & Beans
107 Iguana Burger Hut
105 Piles o' Pizza
108 Yams-on-a-Stick

GOODIES

202 Choc-It-Up
212 Hine's Gourmet Ketchups
103 Jelly Bean Jungle
113 The Lollipop Stop
110 Pickle Palace

SHOES

116 Hoof & Mouth: Shoes & Orthodontia
208 Shoes by Imelda

SPORTING GOODS & TOYS

201 Dodgeball Depot
117 Have You Lost Your Marbles?
114 Jump & Juggle
214 Kickball Korner
205 Hopscotch
206 Toys 4 Us
101 Watch the Birdie: Badminton Outfitter

555-6324

555-4467

555-5299

555-6829

555-5417

"Whoa!" says Dimble. "A multitude of masses! A mass of multitudes!"

"Yikes!" says Laggin. "Too many people!"

"Well, now they've stumped us," says Dimble. "We'll never find them in this crowd. We don't even know what they look like. Might as well head back."

"Let me guess, Eyeballs," says Laggin. "We shouldn't give up yet. You think we can solve this problem, too."

"That's the attitude, Officer Laggin," you say. "It won't be easy to find Rancid and Ruth in this crowd, but it's certainly not impossible. We have lots of useful information, and we did such a good job locating the right platform quickly that we should have enough time."

You pull out your notes on the evidence collected at the apartment.

"I brought the old photo of them that was on the mantle," you say. "And here is a list of clues to their current appearance. Finally, we should remember that they

probably have the ransom items with them. Let's split up, and start looking for these guys."

Moments later, you spot them! "Dimble! Laggin! Over here!" you shout.

 Use the clues to determine what Rancid Roach and Ruth Less-Roach look like. Then use those eyeballs, Eyeballs, to pick them out from the multitude of masses. When you've found them, check the baggage claim numbers on their suitcases. Add them together to determine the next page you want.

Hawaii last winter

The Spittsburgh Science Center

"Where Science Is Everything It's Cracked Up to Be"

1 Science Theater
A spectacular large-screen cinema and a high-tech lecture hall. Check info board for times.

2 Invention and Experiment Station
Come explore the world of inventions and inventors. Help us conduct experiments in physics, chemistry, and psychology. Who knows? Maybe you'll be the next Einstein—or the next Frankenstein!

3 Junior Science Labs
Hands-on science for small fry and bigger fry. Join us as we explore everything from crayons to computers, magic to magnets, spit-up to splashdowns.

4 Egg Drop Center
Every day we scramble more eggs than all the diners in Spittsburgh combined! Come try your hand at designing a vessel to cushion an egg falling three stories onto hard cement. Successful designs are displayed on our Wall of Fame, and designers can sign their names to our Humpty Dumpty Mural, created by artist Scott Polena. You can observe the "egg droppings" on every floor!

5 Biology Center
Any guesses how Jack managed to grow that amazing beanstalk? Come try your hand at developing equally amazing hybrids—or dissect a worm, or map someone's DNA. This place has life!

6 The Cave
If we haven't yet scared you into loving science, then you must visit our cave. Bump into stalactites and trip over stalagmites—or is it the other way around? Learn about bats and other cave dwellers. Cap off your visit with a ride into the *real* (no kidding) coal mine that the Science Center was built over. Hope you like the dark!

Admission
Adults.........$6.00
Children $4.00
Under 2 ....Free
Members ......Free

Key
● Exhibit Areas
● Visitor Services

See back of brochure for more exhibit descriptions. Offices and classrooms are located in the basement.

First Floor

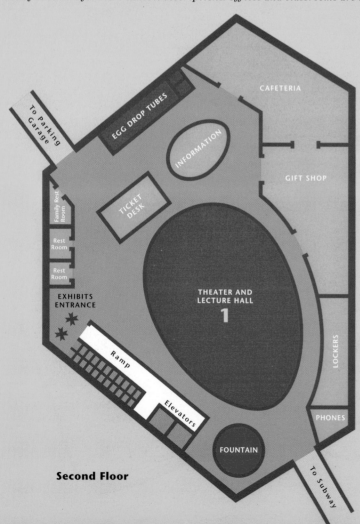

Second Floor

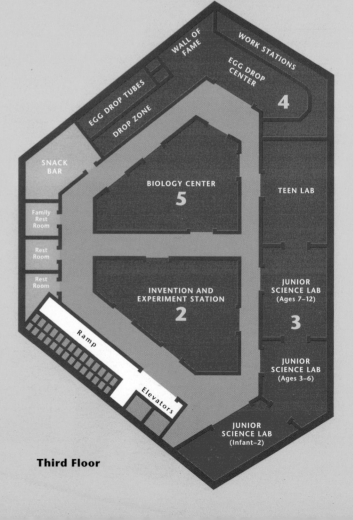

Third Floor

THE RANSOM DROP

LOCKER #26

THE COMPUTER CENTER

THE CAVE
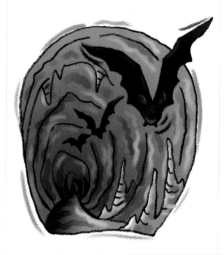

3RD FLOOR REST ROOM

THE EGG DROP CENTER
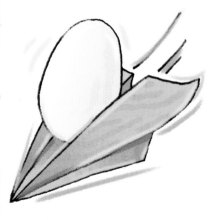

LOCKER #47

You leave the subway and find yourself at the Spittsburgh Science Center! As the petnappers instructed, you buy an admission ticket and go to the Information Desk. You ask whether there has been a message left for "Smartypants." The lady hands you a sealed envelope (and gives you a funny look).

You pull out the next message. It says:

> Good work, Smartypants. Now see if you can do this without messing up.
> 1. Enter the Exhibits Entrance Ramp on this floor. Go down one floor. Exit ramp and turn left.
> 2. After you pass the third rest room, enter the next room on your left through the nearest door. Exit immediately through the far door. Turn right.
> 3. Enter first door on left; exit to corridor through farthest door.
> 4. Enter nearest room. You will find the next set of instructions in the planter in the far right corner.
> Any funny business or any sign of the cops, and you can look for Snookums at your local Iguana Burger Hut. We mean business!!!!!

You get going promptly, wishing you had time to explore the museum. But time is ticking away (and the ransom bag is getting heavy). You grab a science-center guide to help you plan your route.

Follow the petnappers' directions using the floor plan.
Then lift the flap showing the last room you entered.
Be sure to double-check your destinations: some of the flaps are tricks.

TO CATCH SOME THIEVES?

VENEZUELA
LANGUAGE - Spanish
AREAS TO CONSIDER: Caracas, Margarita Is., Barcelona
ADVANTAGES: Great climate, beaches. Shopping excellent.
DISADVANTAGES: Lots of fauna inland. Crackdown on pick-pockets recently.

BRAZIL
LANGUAGE - Portuguese
AREAS TO CONSIDER: São Paulo, Brasilia, Rio de Janeiro
ADVANTAGES: Good beaches. Many wealthy (and careless!) tourists.
DISADVANTAGES: Wildlife to excess.

ARGENTINA
LANGUAGE - Spanish
AREAS TO CONSIDER: Patagonia, Buenos Aires, La Plata
ADVANTAGES: Climate is mild. Good beaches, shopping. Tango! (Maybe some shoplifting?)
DISADVANTAGES: Wildlife abundant.

Map labels: GUYANA, SURINAM, FRENCH GUIANA, VENEZUELA, COLUMBIA, BRAZIL, PERU, BOLIVIA, PARAGUAY, PACIFIC OCEAN, ARGENTINA, CHILE, URUGUAY, ATLANTIC OCEAN

Officer Dimble surveys the list of evidence you've found. "Good thing you suggested a search, Eyeballs," he says. "It's just too bad we arrived too late to apprehend the perps. Maybe we'll catch up with them when they return. Might as well head back for now."

"I'm not so sure it's too late," you say. "I'm going to the deli downstairs to call Ms. B. She might have some suggestions about where to look next."

You ask to borrow a couple of pieces of the evidence, then hurry down to the pay phone. You reach Ms. B. on your first try!

"You have some Grade-A gray matter, Eyeballs," says Ms. B. "I'm also impressed by your persistence. Read me the clues, and we'll make a list of the ones that may help uncover Rancid and Ruth's plans."

"I've already sorted through the clues," you say. "I put them in categories as we uncovered them."

"Such nimble neurons!" says Ms. B., obviously pleased with you. "Organizing a jumble of information is the key to making sense of it. Now, tell me about the evidence."

"There were two clues I thought might help us to figure out their plans," you say. "The first clue is a map of South America that was hanging in their bedroom. There are lists of travel information tacked up next to three of the countries. So, my hypothesis is that they are planning to visit one of these South American countries."

"Your cortex is cooking!" says Ms. B. "Hang on to the map and the notes for a minute. What's the other clue?"

"I haven't really looked at it yet," you say. "I found an envelope from a travel agent postmarked in July. It's labeled 'Possible Itineraries.' I grabbed it because I'm pretty sure that an itinerary is a plan for a trip, isn't it?"

"Yes!" says Ms. B. "Open it right away! Anything inside?"

You unfold the enclosed letter and begin reading it to Ms. B.:

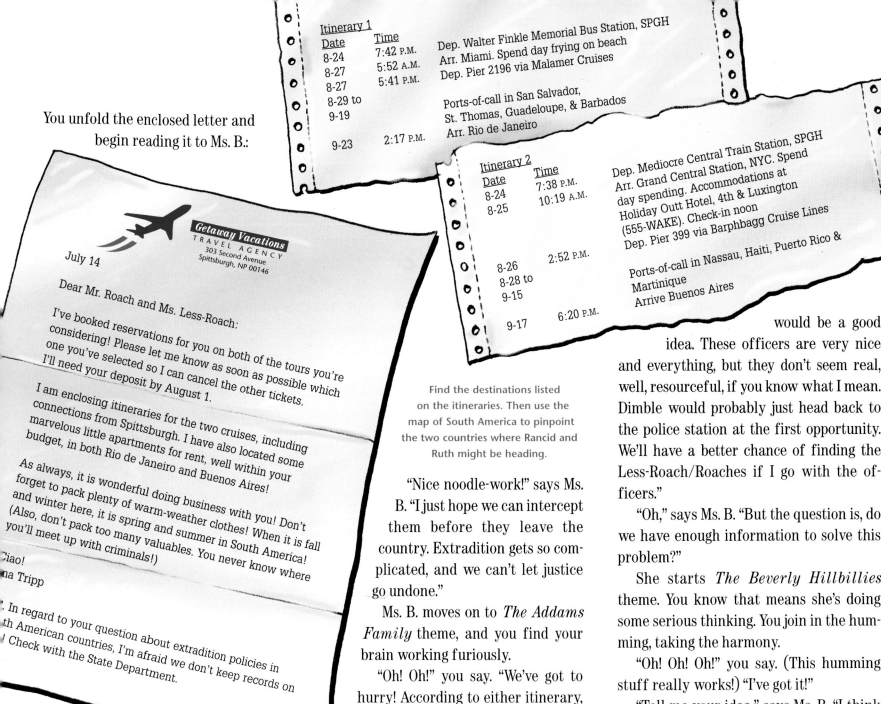

Itinerary 1

Date	Time	
8-24	7:42 P.M.	Dep. Walter Finkle Memorial Bus Station, SPGH
8-27	5:52 A.M.	Arr. Miami. Spend day frying on beach
8-27	5:41 P.M.	Dep. Pier 2196 via Malamer Cruises
8-29 to 9-19		Ports-of-call in San Salvador, St. Thomas, Guadeloupe, & Barbados. Arr. Rio de Janeiro
9-23	2:17 P.M.	

Itinerary 2

Date	Time	
8-24	7:38 P.M.	Dep. Mediocre Central Train Station, SPGH
8-25	10:19 A.M.	Arr. Grand Central Station, NYC. Spend day spending. Accommodations at Holiday Outt Hotel, 4th & Luxington (555-WAKE). Check-in noon
8-26	2:52 P.M.	Dep. Pier 399 via Barphbagg Cruise Lines
8-28 to 9-15		Ports-of-call in Nassau, Haiti, Puerto Rico & Martinique
9-17	6:20 P.M.	Arrive Buenos Aires

Getaway Vacations
TRAVEL AGENCY
303 Second Avenue
Spittsburgh, NP 00146

July 14

Dear Mr. Roach and Ms. Less-Roach:

I've booked reservations for you on both of the tours you're considering! Please let me know as soon as possible which one you've selected so I can cancel the other tickets. I'll need your deposit by August 1.

I am enclosing itineraries for the two cruises, including connections from Spittsburgh. I have also located some marvelous little apartments for rent, well within your budget, in both Rio de Janeiro and Buenos Aires!

As always, it is wonderful doing business with you! Don't forget to pack plenty of warm-weather clothes! When it is fall and winter here, it is spring and summer in South America! (Also, don't pack too many valuables. You never know where you'll meet up with criminals!)

Ciao!
na Tripp

. In regard to your question about extradition policies in th American countries, I'm afraid we don't keep records on Check with the State Department.

"Rats!" you say. "I was hoping this letter would have the answer to our problem. But the itineraries don't even mention any South American countries."

"Hm hm hm-hm," says Ms. B., humming the theme song from *The Brady Bunch.*

"Oh!" you say. (Ms. B.'s humming technique is even starting to work on you.) "Of course! We can use the map to figure out the countries where these cities are. Then we'll be down to two possibilities."

Find the destinations listed on the itineraries. Then use the map of South America to pinpoint the two countries where Rancid and Ruth might be heading.

"Nice noodle-work!" says Ms. B. "I just hope we can intercept them before they leave the country. Extradition gets so complicated, and we can't let justice go undone."

Ms. B. moves on to *The Addams Family* theme, and you find your brain working furiously.

"Oh! Oh!" you say. "We've got to hurry! According to either itinerary, Rancid and Ruth should still be in Spittsburgh! It's 6:45, and the train doesn't leave until 7:38. The bus leaves even later, at 7:42. So if we can figure out their destination, we'll know whether they're at the bus station or the train station. And then we can have the police arrest them!"

"We could just send one officer to the bus station and one to the train station," says Ms. B. "Then it won't matter whether we know their destination."

"Uh, Ms. B.," you say, "I'm not sure that would be a good idea. These officers are very nice and everything, but they don't seem real, well, resourceful, if you know what I mean. Dimble would probably just head back to the police station at the first opportunity. We'll have a better chance of finding the Less-Roach/Roaches if I go with the officers."

"Oh," says Ms. B. "But the question is, do we have enough information to solve this problem?"

She starts *The Beverly Hillbillies* theme. You know that means she's doing some serious thinking. You join in the humming, taking the harmony.

"Oh! Oh! Oh!" you say. (This humming stuff really works!) "I've got it!"

"Tell me your idea," says Ms. B. "I think I've solved this problem, too."

"Well," you say, "I think one of the ransom items may be an important clue to their destination. They wanted a *Spanish-English* dictionary! I think I can tell where we should search for them."

Where in South America are Rancid and Ruth going? If you figured out the two possibilities earlier, you can use this clue and the map to tell which one they selected.

Then look at the correct itinerary. From which station do they depart? Find that station on the street map, and turn to the page indicated.

29

WITH WORK TO DO

Ms. B. welcomes you warmly when at long last you stumble through the door at 622 Teddy Lane. "Would you like something to eat, dearie?" she asks. "You need to nourish those splendid cerebral cells."

Eat? No problem. Ms. B. holds out a large platter of pasta—her version of brain food. You wolf it ravenously, not even stopping to pick out those icky ... whatever-veggies-they-are. Ms. B. sits quietly until you have finished eating.

"There now. I'm sure you feel much better. All ready to finish up our work here before you go home."

Finish up? "Couldn't it wait until morning, Ms. B.?" you ask, yawning. "I'm late. It'll be my turn to be fish food if I don't get home soon."

"A good detective wraps up each case promptly," says Ms. B. "And I've already arranged everything for you. You'll take a taxi home when we're done."

You sigh. "Okay, what's left?"

"We need to type up our report," says Ms. B., fingers poised over the computer keyboard. "You dictate, and I'll type."

When you finish, Ms. B. prints out copies of the report. She hands you an envelope and a large bowl of triple chocolate fudge chunk ice cream. Much better than pistachio.

"This copy is for your files, dear. Nice, clear report. Read it over and make sure everything is accurate."

"Looks perfect. I like the changes you've made. Thanks," you say. "And it does feel good to have all the details wrapped up. Time to call the taxi now."

Pull out the report. (You'll have to get your own ice cream.) The report contains the solutions for each step of the mystery. How'd you do, Eyeballs? I know, you must have done great, or you'd never have navigated yourself to this point.

"Just another minute, dear," Ms. B. says, ignoring your groans.

She hands you two pieces of paper. "One item's from me, and Scari Stori dropped off the other, along with your bike."

Well, now! This is great! Sometimes hard work does pay off! "Way cool certificate! I'll put it up on the fridge. And I never thought I'd get a reward!" you say.

"Ms. Stori was very grateful to have Snookums returned unharmed. I also had a call from Officer Laggin just before you returned. She said that when they got back to the station, they ran some computer checks. Apparently, Rancid and Ruth have been running this petnapping scheme for some time. They don't like the cold winters in Spittsburgh, so they've used ransom money to finance long vacations in warm climates. When they were confronted with the evidence you found in their apartment, they confessed to the petnappings of Snookums and ten other pets. Once they're convicted, there will be even more reward money from some of the other pet owners. Superior sleuthing, Eyeballs!"

A few minutes later, you and your faithful bike head out to the taxi, worn-out and mapped-out. Ms. B. calls out, "See you tomorrow at 9:00 A.M. sharp! We have to fill out the expense account form for our bill. Then at 9:30, a reporter from the *Spittsburgh Times* is coming by. Oh, and a new client is coming in at 10!"

Well! Dimble and Laggin can certainly move quickly and decisively when the time is right! Within seconds, Dimble is handcuffing Rancid and Ruth, and Laggin is reading them their rights.

"No way you could have caught us," Rancid is saying. "We did everything just right. We didn't make any mistakes. How do you know we kidnapped that overgrown salamander? We wouldn't have taken him if someone had begged us to! Why, he chewed our apartment half to pieces! He ate us out of fridge and freezer! Besides, we've never even heard of iguanas before. It wasn't us!"

"Oh, be quiet, Rancid," says Ruth. "How did you finger us, coppers?"

"Let's just say some little eyeballs told us," says Laggin, winking at you.

"You!" says Ruth. "You're the Dweebnik! The Smartypants! The Birdbrain! Oooooh! I should have known you weren't as dumb as you look."

Hey! That sounds like an insult. But never mind. Your stomach is rumbling. Pistachio ice cream or no pistachio ice cream, you haven't done enough eating lately. You thank Dimble and Laggin for their help.

"You were awesome, Eyeballs," says Laggin. "Thanks to you, Spittsburgh will be a much safer place for pets."

"Yeah, guess we wouldn't have made this arrest without you and Ms. B.," says Dimble. "Thanks for everything. Want to come back to the police station with us?"

"No, thanks," you say. "I've got to head back to the office. But I'll be in touch to testify. And to give you navigation lessons."

You direct them to the police station. Now off to Ms. B.'s—and dinner. All you need is the map and your tired feet.

Ugh! Ms. B.'s house is far! Maybe you need the subway map and a token, too.

Okay, you brilliant detective, you. Do you remember where you work? Well, it has been a long, hard day, and you are rather hungry. If you're stuck, try thinking back to the first step of the mystery: the journey from Ms. B.'s to the mall. Can you remember about where you started? If so, look around in the general area for a familiar street name.

Or, if your sense of direction has just let you down, check the address back on p. 5. (After all, good navigators use any resources they can.)

Locate Ms. B.'s house on the map and find the nearby subway stops. Plan the *shortest* journey that gets you to one of these stations. Count the number of stops (*not* including the one where you get on). *Add* this to the number printed by Ms. B.'s house to find the next page in the book. Time to wrap things up!

TIPS ON TURNING: RIGHT AND LEFT

Messing up turns—turning right when you meant to turn left, and vice-versa—is probably the #1 navigational mistake. Here are some tips on becoming a Tip-Top Turner:

1. *Turn the map to match the way you are traveling.*

In other words, if you are heading east on a street, turn the map so that east is at the top. Then right is right, and left is left.

This method can create problems if you have a large map and a tight space, or if you are taking a trip involving many turns. You might find yourself getting tangled, or poking passersby in the eye. So, instead you could:

2. *Remember these rules:*

If you are traveling:

- toward the top of the map, rights and lefts are normal;

- toward the bottom, turn the opposite—right is left and left is right;

- right to left, right is toward the top, left is toward the bottom;

- left to right, right is toward the bottom, left is toward the top.

MORE TIPS ON TURNING: NORTH, SOUTH, EAST, AND WEST

Suppose you're heading north on Burp St. Your instructions say to turn east onto Sneeze Ave. Which way do you turn? If you don't know, here are some clues for conquering compass direction problems (by the way, turn right onto Sneeze):

1. Double-check the compass rose.

Usually, North will be toward the top. But not always! If, for example, the map is oriented with North toward the bottom, and you don't know it, you might head south by accident. (But no matter where North is, East will always be to the right of it, West to the left, and South opposite.)

2. Learn the in-between directions.

Sometimes you'll be instructed to go northeast (NE), or even to find something that is north-northeast (NNE). These terms refer to directions between the standard compass directions. Northeast, for example is halfway between north and east. North-northeast is halfway between north and northeast. Where would west-northwest be? (Halfway between west and northwest.)

EVEN MORE TIPS ON TURNING: CLOCKWISE AND COUNTER

When traveling around the perimeter, or outside edge of an area, you can move clockwise or counterclockwise. Here's how you do that:

1. *Picture the area as a large clock.*

You can do this even if the area isn't actually circular; just pretend it's a funky clock. Locate yourself within that area at the appropriate "o'clock."

2. *Moving clockwise.*

Move toward the higher numbers (up to 12, then start over with 1). In other words, move the same way the hands of a clock do.

3. *Moving counterclockwise.*

Move toward the lower numbers (down to 1, then start over with 12). In other words, move the opposite way the hands of a clock do.

LAST TIPS ON TURNING: TURNING BY DEGREES

To "turn 90 degrees," do you need a thermometer? No! Just do a quarter turn.

A compass circle is divided into 360 degrees (360°). Each quarter turn is therefore 90° (360 ÷ 4 = 90). If you are facing North, and you turn 90° to the right, you'll face east; if you turn 90° to the left, you'll face west.

If you want to face where your backside used to be, turn 180°. "Doing a 360" means you turn all the way around in a circle, ending up facing the way you started.

GIVING AND RECEIVING DIRECTIONS

1. *Remember this rule: More is better.*

Give or get as many details as possible. Useful details include:

- Distinctive landmarks (like "the building that looks like a pickle")

- Approximate distances ("about a mile" or "2 blocks")

- street names ("turn right onto Upchuck St.")

- Compass directions ("East on Eggplant Dr.")

2. *Use abbreviations or symbols when writing directions.*

Here are some common ones:

- R = right
- L = left
- p = past
- St = street
- Ln = Lane
- Dr = Drive
- Ct = Court
- Av or Ave = Avenue
- ➜ = "to" or "toward"

- E = east
- W = west
- N = north
- S = south
- Hwy = Highway
- Rd = Road
- Blvd = Boulevard

Many words can be shortened by leaving out the vowels (like, Pntlss Prk = Pointless Park) or by writing the first part of the word (like, Hosp. = hospital).

DIRECTIONS IN REVERSE

1. *Remember this rule: Tricky, tricky, tricky.*

Reversing directions, especially without a map, is often more difficult than you expect. There are several reasons for this:

- You need to do the opposite of what you did before. If you turned right onto Upchuck, you'll turn left off of it.

- You may not be able to use information that helped you on the way there.

Landmarks that signaled a coming turn may not be visible heading back. For example, if your directions said to turn left 2 blocks past the Giant Lips, you wouldn't be able to see the Giant Lips on the way back until after you'd made the turn, so that landmark wouldn't help you find your way back. Similarly, directions like "go till the St. dead-ends, then turn R" will help only in that you will be looking for a street to the left that doesn't continue—and there might be lots of them.

2. *What to Do:*

When you know that you're likely to have to retrace your steps, here's how to make your task easier:

- Use a map. If possible, mark your route.

- Keep a list of landmarks just past each turn. Look for these on the way back.

- Write down street names and/or distances.

- Write out the reverse directions before you get started, so you'll at least recognize the tricky places in advance.

BALLPARK LOCATIONS

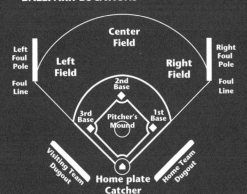